THIS CANDLEWICK BOOK BELONGS TO:

_____

_____

_____

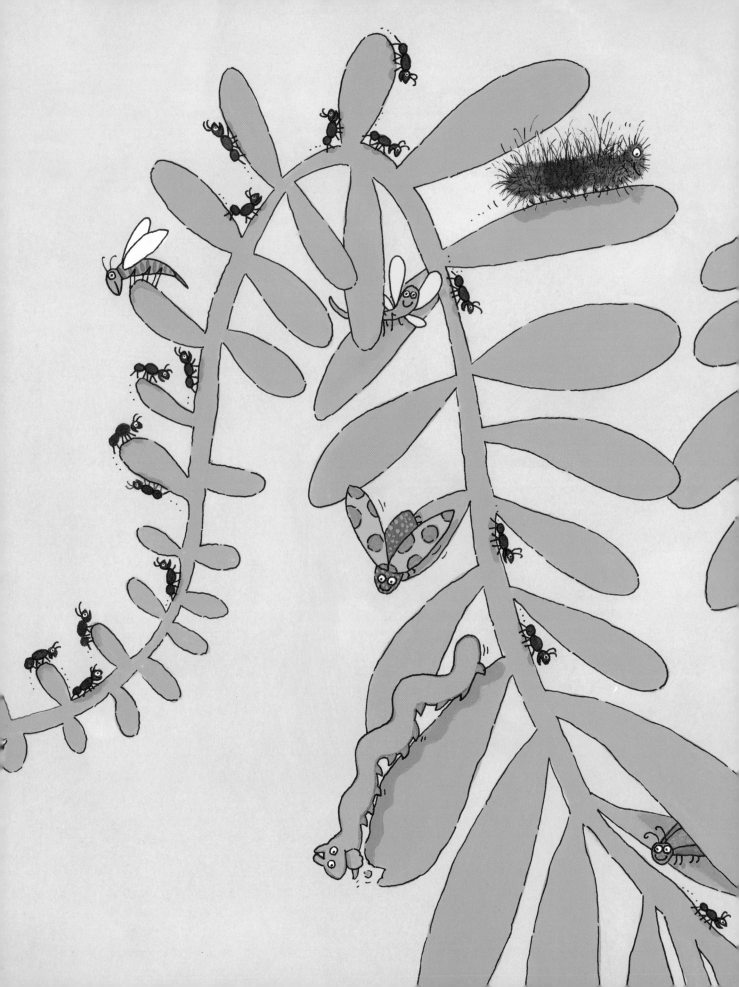

For Dorothy, William, and Nicholas
K. A.

For Connor and Aidan
N. B. W.

Text copyright © 2007 by Katherine Ayres
Illustrations copyright © 2007 by Nadine Bernard Westcott

First paperback edition 2008

The Library of Congress has cataloged the hardcover edition as follows:

Ayres, Katherine.
Up, down, and around / Katherine Ayres ; illustrated by Nadine Bernard Wescott. — 1st ed.
p. cm.
Summary: A garden produces a variety of edible plants, such as corn that grows up,
onions that grow down, and tomato vines that twine all around.
ISBN 978-0-7636-2378-4 (hardcover)
[1. Gardening—Fiction. 2. English language—Prepositions—Fiction. 3. Stories in rhyme.]
I. Westcott, Nadine Bernard, ill. II. Title. III. Title: Up, down, and around.
PZ8.3.A957Up 2007
[E]—dc22   2006049576

ISBN 978-0-7636-4017-0 (paperback)

2 4 6 8 10 9 7 5 3

Printed in Mexico

This book was typeset in Beta bold.
The illustrations were done in ink and watercolor.

Candlewick Press
2067 Massachusetts Avenue
Cambridge, Massachusetts 02140

visit us at www.candlewick.com

UP, DOWN, AND AROUND

Katherine Ayres

illustrated by
Nadine Bernard Westcott

CANDLEWICK PRESS
CAMBRIDGE, MASSACHUSETTS

In the dirt we'll dig a row,
drop some seeds, and watch them grow.

Dirt piles up;
seeds
go
down.

Water splashes
around and around.

Corn grows up.

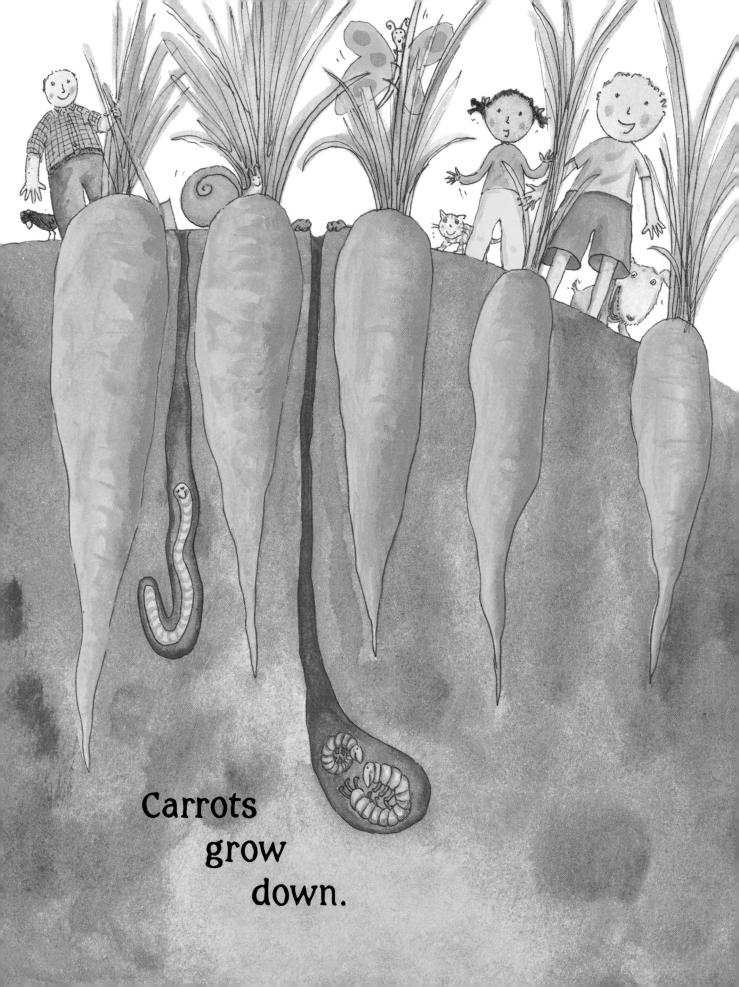

Carrots
grow
down.

cucumbers climb
around and around.

Peppers grow up.

Potatoes
      grow
            down.

pumpkins vine around and around.

Broccoli grows up.

Beets
grow
down.

Green beans wind
around and around.

Okra grows up.

Onions
grow
down.

Tomatoes twine around and around.

Fresh and tasty,
get a bunch.

Pick some.
Pull some.

LET'S HAVE LUNCH!

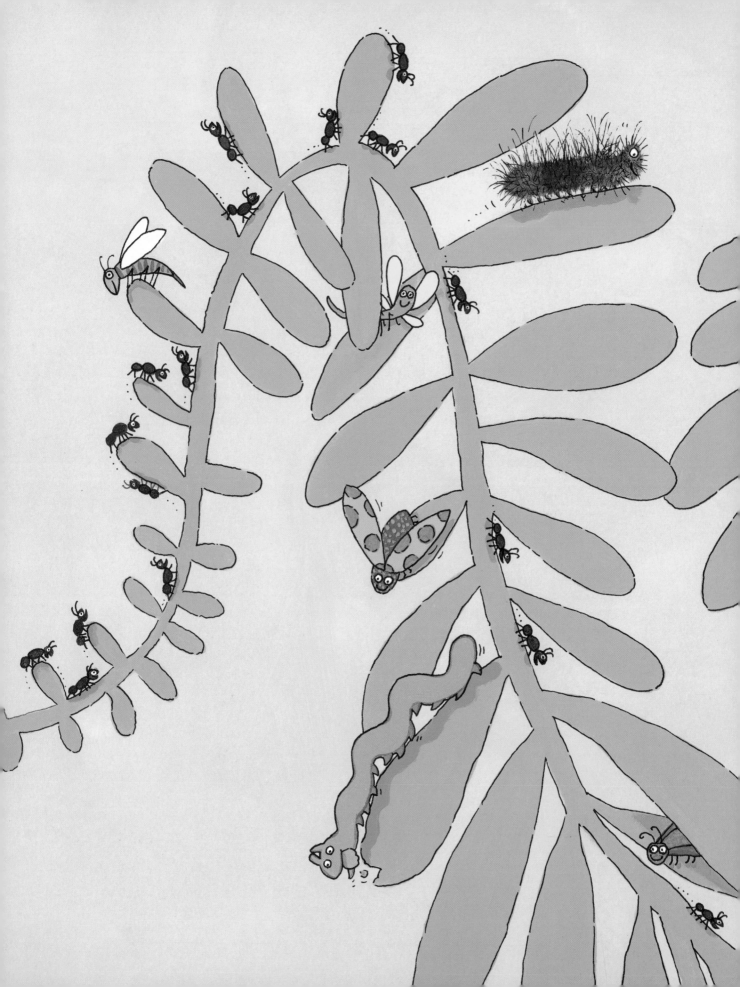

Katherine Ayres is the author of *A Long Way*, illustrated by Tricia Tusa, and *Matthew's Truck*, illustrated by Hideko Takahashi. About this book, she says, "To me as a child, strawberries equaled summer. The best dinners were those with sweet corn and tomatoes fresh from my grandfather's garden. He loved growing all sorts of plants, and so do I." Katherine Ayres lives in Pennsylvania.

Nadine Bernard Westcott has illustrated more than a hundred books for children. *Up, Down, and Around* reminds her of the garden her husband plants every year: "It starts out OK in the spring, but by the end of the summer, the squash, ornamental gourds, and pumpkins have taken over!" Nadine Bernard Westcott lives on Nantucket Island.